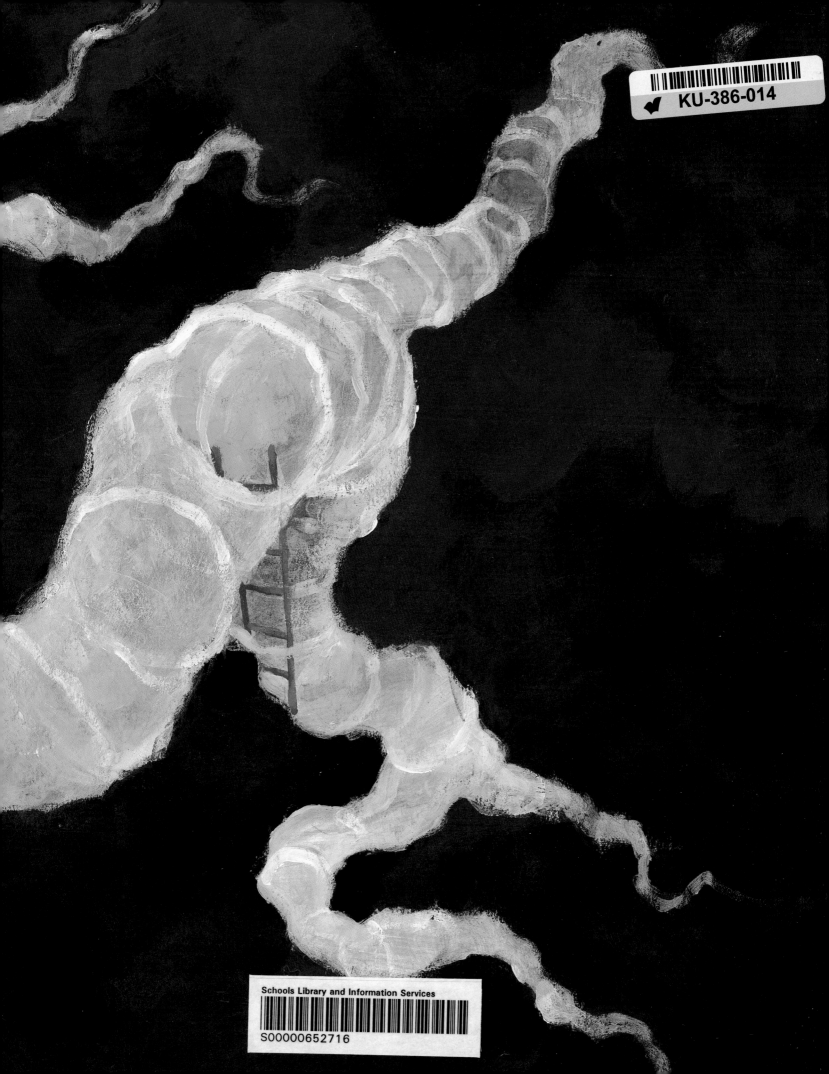

First published in the United States, Great Britain, Canada, Australia, and New Zealand
in 2004 by North-South Books, an imprint of Nord-Süd Verlag AG, Gossau Zürich, Switzerland.

Distributed in the United States by North-South Books Inc., New York.

Library of Congress Cataloging-in-Publication Data is available.
A CIP catalogue record for this book is available from The British Library.
ISBN 0-7358-1879-7 (trade edition) 10 9 8 7 6 5 4 3 2 1
ISBN 0-7358-1880-0 (library edition) 10 9 8 7 6 5 4 3 2 1
Printed in Italy

For more information about our books, and the authors and artists
who create them, visit our web site: www.northsouth.com

E. T. W. Igel

Mole's Journey

Illustrated by Jakob Kirchmayr

Translated by Sibylle Kazeroid

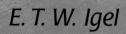

A Michael Neugebauer Book
North-South Books
New York · London

Ah . . . achoo! Mole had caught a cold.
Feeling miserable, he trudged home. He'd been at Owl's house,
hearing all about Owl's recent trip. "I'd like to take a trip, too!"
Mole grumbled. *Ah . . . achoo!*

When he got home, he was shivering—chilled to
the bone. He filled his hot water bottle, then he
got right into bed. As Mole snuggled under the
covers he thought about the trip he wanted to take—
a trip all the way around the world!

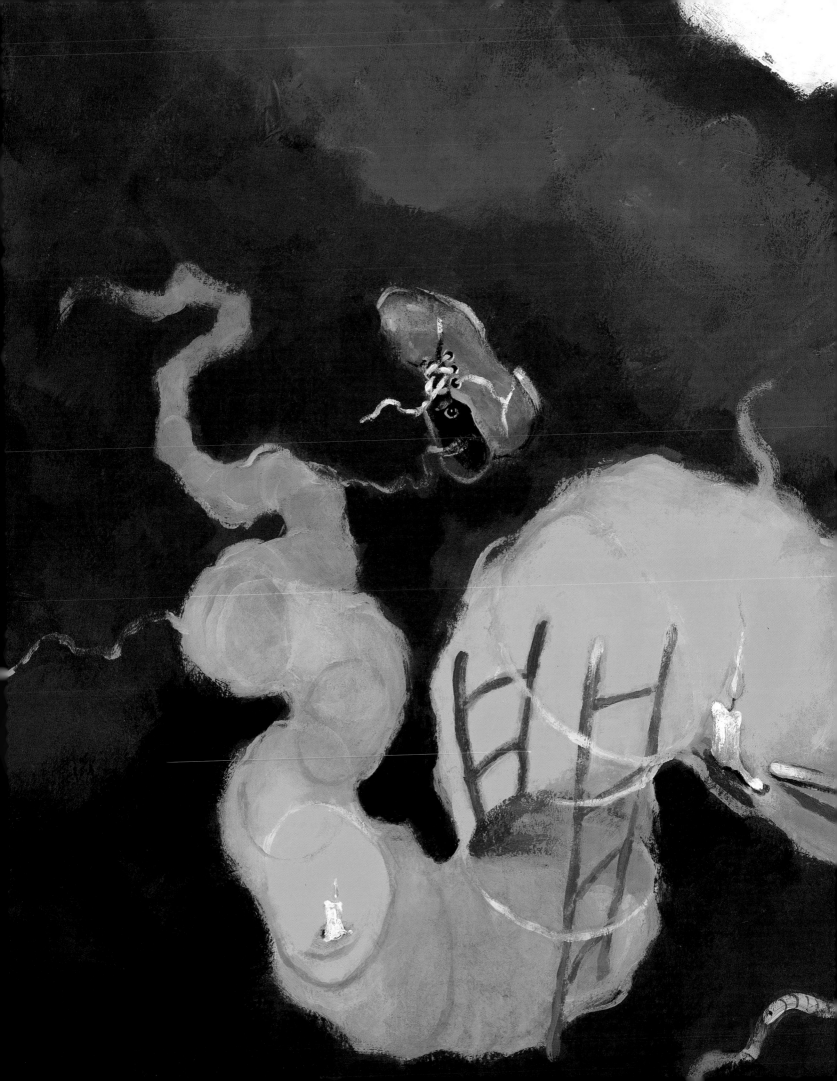

"That's it!" he said. "My mind is made up." Mole jumped out of bed, grabbed
his shovel, went into his tunnel, and began digging. He dug and dug
without stopping. He had never dug so much in his life.
Finally he dug his way to the surface and . . .

. . . he popped out of the tunnel onto the ground. Or rather, onto the ice.
My, is it cold! thought Mole. He looked around and was startled to see
a big white bear sitting in front of him.
"Where did you just come from?" asked the bear. Mole told him everything.
"And where am I now?" he asked
"At the North Pole, of course!" said the bear.
"I dug that far?" exclaimed Mole.

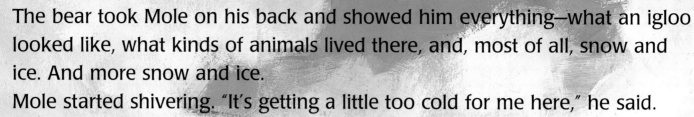

The bear took Mole on his back and showed him everything—what an igloo looked like, what kinds of animals lived there, and, most of all, snow and ice. And more snow and ice.

Mole started shivering. "It's getting a little too cold for me here," he said. "Thanks for the tour." Then he said good-bye to the bear and headed back into his tunnel.

It *was* beautiful there, thought Mole. Just too cold!

He began to dig farther.

This time when he reached the
surface he felt very, very warm.
"Where am I now?" he asked.
"In the desert, of course," replied a fox, peering out from behind a tree.
"Where did you come from?"
"From the North Pole," declared Mole proudly. And he told
the fox about his trip around the world.
"You arrived just in time," said
the fox. "A camel race is
about to start; you can
join it if you want."

Of course Mole wanted to. Because he was a special guest, he was given the fastest camel. How thrilled Mole was to win first prize—a shiny new shovel!

"Very practical," said Mole happily. "I've wanted a new shovel for a long time!" But it was just too hot for him in the desert, so he said good-bye to the fox and headed back into his tunnel.

Mole got busy digging again. When he finally reached the surface
he had to break through thick rock.
When he looked out, he saw many mountains with snowcapped peaks.
Achoo! Mole sneezed. Then he heard a shrill whistle.
It was a groundhog who was frightened by Mole.
But he came closer, curious. He even invited Mole into his burrow.
"Thank you very much," said Mole, "but the air up here is
so dry that my throat is all scratchy and it's a little hard to breathe. I
don't feel so well and I think I should go home."

Mole jumped into his tunnel and dug some more.
But when he came to the surface again, he still
wasn't home. Instead he was somewhere terribly warm
and humid.
"Look," said a parrot who sat on a branch above Mole, "a
mole. But you don't belong in this jungle. Where did you
come from?"
"I'm on a trip around the world!" said Mole. "Actually,
I want to go home, but I must have dug
the wrong way."

The parrot showed Mole the other animals in the jungle and of course the jungle itself, which was very big, very green, and very humid. The air was so thick and wet that Mole's nose got all stuffed up.
Mole longed to go home to his own forest.

". . . always too hot or too cold, too dry or too wet," mumbled Mole—and then he opened his eyes. He was lying in his bed, and Owl, Squirrel, and Badger were sitting around him.

"What are you doing here?" asked Mole.

"You were sick," explained Owl, "so we visited you and took care of you. You had a very high fever!"

"But you're much better now," added Squirrel quickly.

"But . . . but there's a new shovel over there," said Mole. "Where did it come from?"

"Well . . . we don't know either," said Badger, laughing.

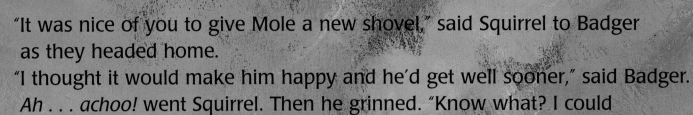

"It was nice of you to give Mole a new shovel," said Squirrel to Badger
as they headed home.
"I thought it would make him happy and he'd get well sooner," said Badger.
Ah . . . achoo! went Squirrel. Then he grinned. "Know what? I could
use a new nutcracker!"

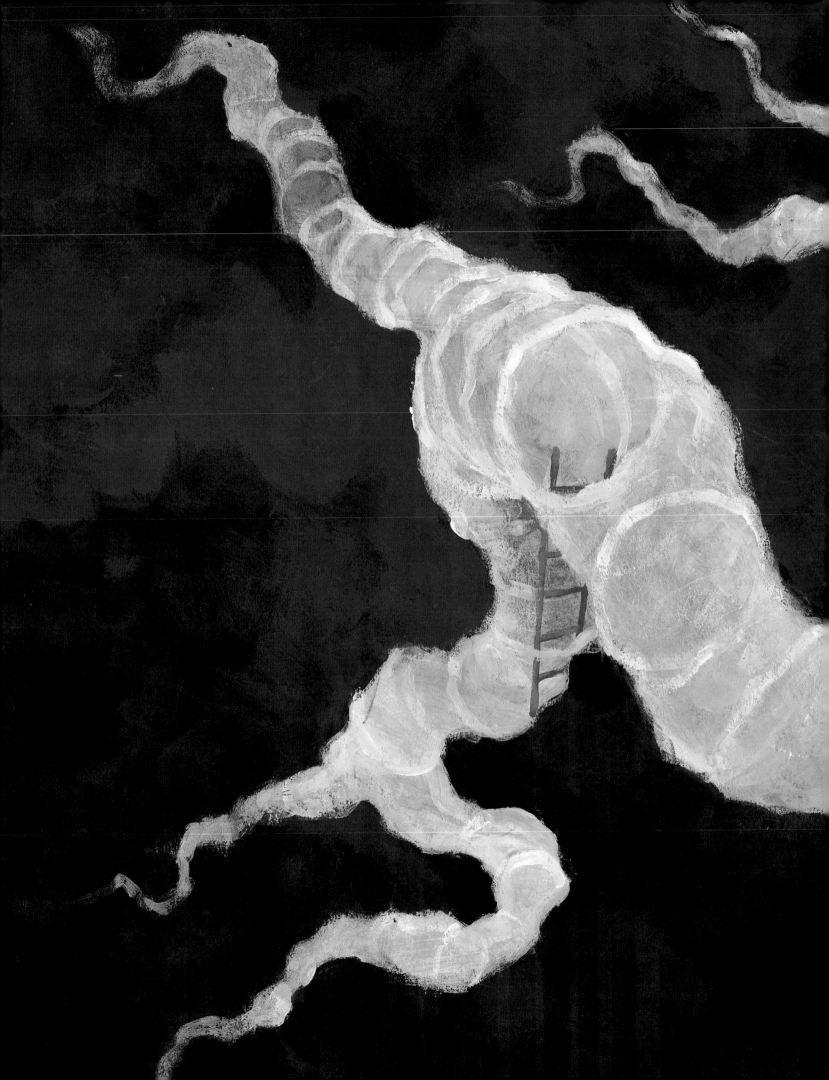